LOOK! BEC IS 95 WITH TAS

KNOWLEDGE BOOKS

MASTERY DECODABLES

What can Gem do?

It is time Tas and Bec came home.

Tas is late.

Bec is late.

Look! Who is it?

It is Brin.

Look! Tas is with Brin.

Look! Bec is with Brin.

Gem can see Tas and Bec.

Tas and Bec are home.

Brin saw Tas and Bec go out of the open gate.

Brin came with Tas and Bec to save them.

Brin can see Tas and Bec are happy in the garden.

Brin can shut the gate.

Gem can see Brin in the garden.

Gem and Brin live in the same street.

Gem is happy to see the gate is shut.

Gem is happy Tas and Bec are home.

Tas and Bec like Brin.

Gem is happy.

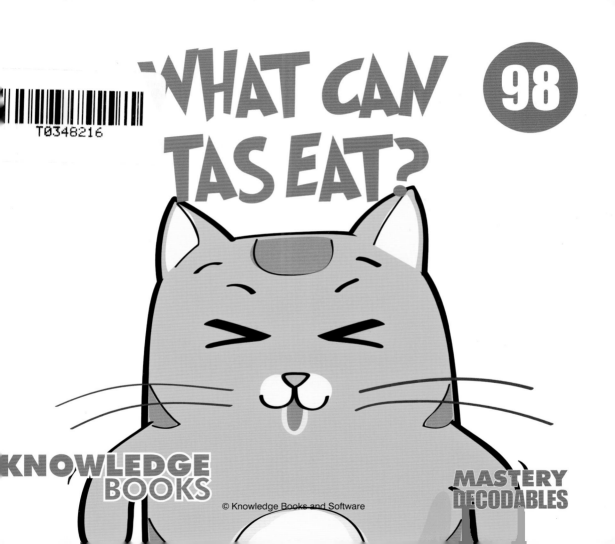

WHAT CAN TAS EAT?

98

On the farm the sheep can eat grain.

Tas could not eat the grain.

Bec could eat the grain.

Bec likes the grain.

Tas does not like the grain.

What can Tas eat?

Look! Brin has food for Tas.

What is it?

Brin has a pie for Tas.

Brin and Tas can eat the pie together.

Tas and Gem are back together.

Bec is back in the shed.

Brin is back on the farm.

Tas, Bec and Brin are happy.

14

Gem is not happy with Tas.

Tas went to the farm garden.

The garden was wet with lots of mud.

Tas is wet and has mud on her coat.

What will Gem do?

Gem will give Tas a bath!